About this book

Many children have difficulty puzzling out letters because they are abstract symbols. Letterland's worldwide success is all about its enduring characters who give these symbols life and stop them from being abstract. In this book we meet Sammy Snake. His story is carefully designed to emphasise the sounds that the letter 'S' makes in words. This definitive, original story book is an instant collector's classic, making learning fun for a new generation of readers.

A TEMPLAR BOOK

This edition published in the UK in 2008 by Templar Publishing
an imprint of The Templar Company plc,
The Granary, North Street, Dorking, Surrey, RH4 1DN, UK
www.templarco.co.uk

First published by Hamlyn Publishing, 1985
Devised and produced by The Templar Company plc

ISBN 978-1-84011-762-2

Printed in China

Letterland © was devised by and is the copyright of Lyn Wendon
LETTERLAND® is a registered trademark

Classic LETTERLAND Storybooks

Sammy Snake and the Snow

Written by
Keith Nicholson & Richard Carlisle

Illustrated by
Jane Launchbury

templar publishing

It was the middle of winter in Letterland and there was snow in the Letterland mountains. Sammy Snake had never seen snow before, so he decided to go and see it for himself.

He put down his suitcase and looked out of the window. What he saw gave him quite a surprise.

Almost straight away he slipped over. "Oops!" cried Sammy. "Snow is ssslippery stuff!" "And cold too," he added as he skidded into a big snowman.

"I'm very sorry, sir," said Sammy, struggling to stay right-side-up. He was a little surprised when the snowman said nothing in reply.

"Is this the way to the ski slopes?" continued Sammy politely. But the snowman just stood there, silent and still.

"Never mind," said Sammy to himself, "I'll find my own way." And off he slithered through the snow.

On the ski slopes everyone was having fun.

"This is sssplendid," hissed Sammy as he watched people swishing past on skis.

Swish! Swoosh! Down the slopes they went – some on skis and some on sledges. Sammy wished he could join in the fun.

Then he saw an empty sledge. So he slid over and scrambled on to it.

"This looks simple," he said to himself and he gave a great big push with his tail. Off went the sledge, sliding down the slope.

Soon the slope became steeper and steeper. The sledge started to go faster and faster.

Within a few seconds Sammy was streaking along.

"How do I steer this thing?" he cried.

He was going so fast that everyone had to jump out of his way!
Even the fastest skiers couldn't keep up!

Sammy thought it would be sensible to slow down a bit. He wasn't sure that he liked going so fast.

He tried swerving from side to side. But that didn't help much.

The he tried closing his eyes. But that didn't slow him down at all!

When he opened his eyes again he could see people standing at the bottom of the slope looking up at him.

"Stop, sledge, ssstop!" hissed Sammy. "Otherwise we will end up going SPLAT!"

By now everyone at the bottom of the slope was watching the sledge speeding towards them.

It was still quite a long way away, so they couldn't see exactly what it was.

The Kicking King thought it was a snowball! Naughty Nick thought it must be something supersonic.
The Quarrelsome Queen thought, whatever it was, it shouldn't be allowed.

"That thing is going much too fast!" she cried. "We must stop it before it smashes into us!"

Then they realised who it was.
"Sammy Snake!" they all cried.

"**W**e'll have to stop him somehow," said the Kicking King. "What *ever* can we do?"

"I'll turn him into a snowstorm!" suggested the Wicked Witch. But no one liked that idea.

"I'll throw snowballs at him!" suggested Naughty Nick. But no one liked that idea either.

Then Fireman Fred suggested something that they all liked. "We'll build a big soft snowman at the bottom of the slope for him to crash into," he said. "That should stop him!"

So they started straight away.

Everyone scooped up piles of snow and started to make a huge snowman. Bigger and bigger it grew, as everyone rushed to add more and more snow.

Soon the snowman was as tall as Eddy Elephant, but a lot softer.

Then they watched as Sammy and his sledge came nearer and nearer.

When Sammy saw the snowman in front of him his eyes opened as wide as saucers.

The snowman was over sixteen feet high.

For a split second he wondered if it was the same silent snowman he had skidded into at the top of the slope? "If it is, he's grown a lot since I last saw him," thought Sammy.

But there was no time to ask – Sammy and the sledge were speeding straight for him!

A moment later Sammy Snake and the sledge went SPLAT, right into the snowman's side. The sledge went spinning and Sammy soared into the air in a great, big somersault.

Soon they both came to land in the soft snow.

Sammy looked round for the snowman but all that was left was a big, sloppy white heap. It didn't look like a snowman at all.

At first Sammy was too startled to speak. He wanted to say "sorry" to the snowman but there was nothing left for him to say "sorry" to.

Soon everyone had gathered round. "Are you all right Sammy?" they asked.

"Yes," he replied sadly, "but I'm afraid the snowman isn't."
"Oh, that's all right," they replied.
"We made it especially for you."

"Oh…" said Sammy slowly.
His eyes opened wide again.
"I ssssee,' he hissed. "It was not a snowMAN… but a SNOWman! Still, I'm sorry I spoilt it for you."

"Never mind," cried everyone.
"Would you like to help us build another one, just for fun?"

"Oh yes please!" hissed Sammy.
So they did.

THE END